A King for Christmas

By:
Brooke St. James

A King for Christmas

Published in Nashville, Tennessee, by Elm Hill, an imprint of Thomas Nelson. Elm Hill and Thomas Nelson are registered trademarks of HarperCollins Christian Publishing, Inc.

Elm Hill titles may be purchased in bulk for educational, business, fund-raising, or sales promotional use. For information, please e-mail SpecialMarkets@ThomasNelson.com.

ISBN 978-1-4003-3480-3

CHAPTER 1

—⟁—

January 1973

Sergeant James Graham
Atlanta, Georgia

*J*ames Graham had been stationed at Fort Benning, Georgia for the past year. His parents and grandparents lived in the panhandle of Florida, and he had some family in Atlanta, so Fort Benning seemed like a good fit.

A while back, a guy by the name of Daniel King came to teach at the base, and the two of them, Daniel and James, became instant friends. They were different, but a lot alike, too. Daniel was fun-loving but he had a serious side. The same was true for James, though his serious side rarely showed. James was voted class clown in high school. He had mellowed out in recent years, but he was still the life-of-the-party type.

He was a master at handling cards, and he liked to deal them and perform tricks. Because of this, action and conversation often centered around him. James had no problem making friends, but he only had a small circle of people he kept close, and Daniel King immediately became one of them. Daniel had a sharp, dry sense of humor, and it complimented James's personality perfectly. The friendship between them was instant and comfortable.

That was why it was a no-brainer that James would make this trip with his friend. It was a big weekend. Daniel's best friend from back home in Texas was a boxer by the name of Billy Castro. Billy had made it to the big time. Tomorrow night, he would fight for a belt that would crown him as the welterweight champion of the world. Daniel would be ringside with the coaches during the match.

As if this wasn't enough excitement for the weekend, Daniel and his girlfriend (now wife), Abby, surprised their families by tying the knot in an old chapel in the woods during a pit stop while they were all traveling to Atlanta for Billy's boxing match. This happened last night, and tomorrow night would be the big match. It was a weekend full of action and surprises.

James had gone to the small wedding ceremony, and had planned on going to the match as well, but Billy Castro threw another proposition out there, and suddenly they got even busier.

Teddy Thomas was a boxing promoter and self-proclaimed "wild man" and he had invited Billy and his friends to his house for a party. He was an Atlanta resident who threw these types of parties several times a year. He told Billy to bring as many guests as he wanted, so Billy mentioned it to everyone who was at the wedding. James had been there to support Daniel, and he had just met Billy, but he wasn't going to pass up an opportunity to go to a party at Teddy Thomas's house. James had an aunt in Atlanta, so he made plans for himself and a couple of friends from the base to spend two nights at her house.

Learning to handle and deal cards was the best decision James had ever made. Whether he was doing a trick or dealing for a game, handling cards put him in the center of the action during social situations, and that was where he loved to be.

He was dealing a hand at the moment.

The whole group met at the hotel in Atlanta where Billy and the rest of his coaches and teammates were staying. It was near the venue where the match would take place. James and the others who had traveled from Fort Benning all met up in Daniel's hotel room in preparation to go to Teddy's party. James dealt a few hands while they were waiting for the women to get dressed. Everybody was in good spirits. Daniel was all excited about getting married, and the rest of them were pumped about the party and Billy's fight.

They went through several hands of blackjack, laughing and cutting up the whole time. The game broke up not long after Daniel's new wife, Abby, and her sister, Tess, came in. Tess was the one who was married to Easy Billy Castro, so it was a big weekend for everyone involved.

Daniel's younger sister came into the room right before they headed out. Laney was her name. Daniel had talked about her a lot in the time that James had been getting to know him. James knew that Laney had been dating a guy named Michael for a long time and that the two of them would be coming to this event together. He had met them both at the wedding last night.

James was taken aback when he met Laney. Daniel's description hadn't done her justice. He wasn't expecting her to be beautiful. Daniel had talked about his sister, but he never mentioned that she was so lovely. Judging by the way he spoke about her as his *little sister*, James expected her to be more of a teenager. He knew she had a long-time boyfriend but he still thought of her as a kid for some reason. Daniel hadn't done a good job of conveying that Laney was a grown woman or that she happened to be gorgeous.

James couldn't let himself look at her. She was with someone else, and apparently, it was serious. Michael Elliott was the guy's name. His family owned a big seafood restaurant in Galveston.

From the start, Michael did his best to become friends with James. He was always up for a good time, and he could see that James was at the center of it, so he was drawn to him. James was annoyed by him, honestly. It wasn't that he had Laney King—it was that he didn't even care—he treated her like she was an afterthought. He didn't know how special she was. Maybe it was that they had been together for so long that Michael was numb to Laney's worth. Regardless, he treated her nonchalantly, and that aggravated James.

James talked to Laney alone several times during the evening, and he always had a good time with her, but his interactions were forced when he was with both of them. Michael desperately wanted to earn James's approval, and James pretended to give it to him just to be nice and maintain the positive vibe of the evening.

James was at Teddy's late into the evening, and he rubbed elbows with a lot of different people, but none of them stood out to him like Laney King. She was a flower in the midst of a bunch of rocks. James wanted to protect her—to surround her. He wanted to shield her from her own boyfriend. That guy didn't deserve her.

But these were all feelings that would go undiscussed.

The two of them had been together for long enough that Laney knew what she was dealing with by now. No one was forcing her to stay with him. James chose to treat them both like he was indifferent about their relationship since he should be indifferent about it.

But it was too much to handle when he saw Michael Elliot talking to another girl like he was interested. It happened twice at Teddy's party. James talked to Laney quite a bit during the course of the night. He liked her and respected her as a person, and it irritated him that Michael didn't love her enough to avoid other girls.

James and Michael were downstairs at the hotel restaurant on the night of the fight when it happened yet again. They had gone down after the match to pick up food for a small celebration in Billy's honor. Room service was taking forever, and the two of them went to check on it.

Michael went off to speak with the girl working the front desk. It was obvious that he wasn't just on hotel business, and James felt like he had ignored it long enough.

It took James a minute to wrap up downstairs, and he had to pry Michael away from the receptionist before they could make their way to the elevator. He knew he was going to say something. The thing was, the receptionist had nothing on Laney. It made James so mad that Michael couldn't see how special she was.

The two of them ended up riding in the elevator with the hotel employee who was taking the room service cart up to their room. It was filled with trays of food. Michael talked to the guy. He was in a good mood, and he made conversation about Billy's match. James told himself to simmer down and leave it alone, but he had seen too much to keep quiet.

"You need to treat your lady better," James said.

There was no mistaking what he said, but Michael turned to James, smiling as if he must have misheard. "What?" he said smiling like he thought James was joking.

"Your lady," James said. "Laney."

"Yeah, what about her?"

"You need to treat her better."

Michael glanced at James. He was smiling at first, but his expression grew serious when he saw that James wasn't smiling. He tilted his head, contemplating what to say. "Or what?" Michael said. There was the hint of a smile on his lips, like he figured James would start laughing and say he was kidding around.

"Or someone else will," James said, straight-faced.

This caused the hotel employee to look their way, widening his eyes a little like he thought there might be trouble. Michael pulled back, staring at James as if trying to figure out his intentions, but then he just smiled and shook his head, leaning back and glancing upward as the elevator moved.

"Laney's not going anywhere," he assured James. "Her whole life revolves around me and the fact that I'm taking over my dad's restaurant. She's gonna help me with that. She's in it for the long haul."

"What's that even mean?" James asked.

Michael shrugged. "It means she depends on me to make her life turn out the way she wants. She's not going anywhere. She quit school already because, what's the point? Everything she needs to know, she can learn by working at the restaurant."

James stared at him. "What school did she quit?"

"College," Michael said, shaking his head casually. "She was studying something useless like history, and I was like *what's the point, Laney*? It's not like she'd do anything with that degree, anyway."

"What does any of that have to do with you talking to other girls?" James asked.

The elevator dinged, and the doors opened. James reached out to hold the door and motioned for the hotel employee to go ahead of them. Michael smirked, not skipping a beat. "I'm just saying… Laney doesn't care if I talk to other girls. She knows she's my main woman."

Michael walked out of the elevator smiling. He was confident and unbothered by the conversation. James figured he had done all he could do. Daniel was a good guy, and if he thought he needed to step in and help his sister, he would. Also, if Laney wanted to marry a man with no self-control, that was her choice. It was their lives, after all, and James figured he had interfered enough.

CHAPTER 2

Laney King

Six months later
Summer
Galveston, Texas

*M*y life was fine. Everything was right on track. I had a lot to be thankful for, and one of the things at the top of the list was my brother, Daniel, and the fact that he would be moving home this weekend. It had been years since he moved away, and I was absolutely chomping at the bit to have him back home.

He had become a man in the time he had been gone. He had endured a lot, including going to war, and the thought of having him home after years of uncertainty felt like a dream come true.

His wife, Abby, had already picked out their new house and was getting settled in it. Now all that was left was for my brother to travel home safely.

This would happen today, thank the Lord.

Two days ago, my dad, along with my boyfriend, Michael, went to Georgia with a truck and small trailer to help Daniel get his things and move back home. I would have gone, too, but they needed all the room they could get since Daniel wasn't renting a moving van. They called when they stopped in Lake Charles for gas. I was already at my brother's house with Abby, helping her hang pictures and do some last-minute cleaning in preparation for his arrival.

Tess was there, too, and so were our mothers, and all five of us went outside when we saw them pull into the driveway.

"Hello! Welcome home!" My mom waved and yelled before the guys even got out of their trucks. My dad was driving Michael's truck and trailer, which he pulled into the driveway.

Daniel parked next to him, and I scanned both vehicles, looking for Michael. I saw him when he sat up. He had been lying back in the passenger's seat of his own truck, and he sat up slowly. He had on a baseball cap and sunglasses, and it looked like there was some discoloration on his cheek and mouth. Maybe it was a shadow. I stared at him, wondering what it was.

Meanwhile, my mother was still next to me, chirping like a bird about how happy she was to have Daniel home. She and

Abby went to my brother's truck before he even had the chance to get out.

I glanced their way, but then I quickly looked at Michael again and watched as he stepped out of his truck. The whole side of his mouth, extending down to his jaw, was purple and looked swollen. I could see that he had been hurt.

"What happened?" I asked as I instantly crossed to him. My brother was standing close by, and I reached out to give him a sideways hug. He had a grasp on his wife and didn't let her go, but he hugged me tightly with one arm. The whole greeting was thrown off because I was distracted by my boyfriend's face. "What in the world happened to you?" I asked again, still staring at him as I broke the hug with my brother.

I moved closer to Michael as we congregated in the driveway, and I could clearly see that he was in bad shape.

"Michael," I said, going up to him. I stood in front of him to get a look at his face, but he pulled away from me, flinching like he was hurt.

"He didn't tell you?" my dad asked.

"I didn't tell her either," Mom said, glancing over her shoulder at me. "Your dad told me there had been a little altercation, but I didn't mention it to you. I honestly didn't think it was that bad. He told me Michael had a black eye."

"He does have a black eye," Dad said.

I reached up for Michael's hat, trying to move it so that I could get a better look at him. He pulled away from me, but he took his sunglasses off impatiently, staring down at me with a smile that was forced.

He looked bad.

"What happened? Who did this to you? Are you okay?"

"I'm fine," he said. "I'm just tired. I was sleeping when we pulled up."

"He went out with some of my buddies from the base last night," Daniel explained. "He got banged up at the pool hall."

"At the pool hall?" I asked. "What were you doing there?"

"Playing pool," Michael said as if that was obvious.

"Your eye," I said, staring at the swollen lump on his eyebrow. "Are you okay? Did you look at your face? Who did this to you? Why would they? Were you with my brother?"

"I wasn't there," Daniel said.

"Why did you let him go out playing pool?" I asked.

"He wanted to go, so he went," my brother said. "He makes his own choices."

"How did this happen?"

"It's not as bad as it looks," Michael assured me.

He was shrugging it off, which seemed crazy. I was stunned. But action kept happening around me. So much was going on around their arrival that for the next hour, we carried boxes and unloaded, and I didn't get to talk to Michael about his face at all.

But I couldn't let it go.

It wasn't just a black eye. There was bruising and swelling around his eye and his mouth. If he had been fighting with a man when this happened, then he had certainly been hit more than once. Michael acted like he wanted to let it go and not discuss it, which was unbelievable to me. I couldn't get past it.

Then to add to it all, Michael tried to sneak away without talking to me. He slipped out after we got everything unpacked. He helped my dad unhitch the trailer, and he decided to up and leave while he was out there. I ran to the driveway to catch him when I saw him driving off. He stopped and rolled the window down.

"Where are you going?" I asked.

"Home," he said. "I'm tired. I need a shower."

"You didn't even tell me you were leaving. I haven't seen you in two days."

"I told your dad I was leaving. He obviously told you."

"Gosh, Michael, what's going on? It's weird that you show up here with your face like that, and then you want to leave without saying goodbye to me. Who did this to you? What happened exactly? You haven't even talked to me about it. Why didn't you tell me?"

"Because, whatever, Laney, maybe I don't want to talk about it. It was just a stupid fight."

"With who?"

"That dude, James. He's just an idiot with a bad temper. He got mad and sucker-punched me because I beat him at pool. It's nothing. Guy stuff. I don't want to talk about it. I already told you this, and you keep coming out here, chasing me down and asking me questions."

"He sucker-punched you?"

"Yes, Laney," Michael said impatiently.

"And he did this to you because you beat him at a *pool game*?"

"Yes. But that's not even the point. It was just a stupid fight. I've been on the road all day, and I'm ready to get home and take a shower."

He drove off with no closure whatsoever, and I walked inside, feeling like I might be sick. *Guy stuff?* Michael had never gotten into a fight before. I couldn't understand why he was just shrugging it off. I went straight to my brother after he left.

"Why would your friend do that to Michael?" was the first thing I asked Daniel when I found him in the kitchen.

He looked at me, smiling a calm, almost apologetic smile as he gave a little shrug. "I don't even know the whole story," Daniel said. "They were out late last night, and Michael was at my house like that when I woke up this morning. I was busy getting on the road, so I didn't talk to him much about it. He didn't seem like he wanted to talk about it, honestly."

"He said James did it," I said.

Daniel nodded calmly. "I know. That's what he said to me, too. I wasn't surprised because that's who he was out with last night."

"Are you talking about your friend, James? The one who deals cards?"

"Yes."

I stared at my brother, blinking, feeling shocked. "You weren't surprised that he beat up my boyfriend? Is it normal for him to beat people up?" I asked.

"No," Daniel said. He blinked and stared at me, unmoving. We were standing in the kitchen, and he was holding onto Abby like he never wanted to let her go again.

"Well, why did he do that?" I asked, since I seemed to be missing something.

"I have no idea, but…" Daniel closed and then opened his mouth, hesitating just the right way where I knew he wanted to say something else.

"But what?" I said.

"I don't know what to tell you," he said reluctantly. "I just know James wouldn't do something like that for no reason."

"Well, neither would Michael," I said, being defensive. "He's never done anything like this before."

"You should just talk to Michael, then," Daniel said.

"He doesn't want to talk about it. He said it was guy stuff."

Daniel made a moaning, stretching noise, holding on to Abby and making it obvious that he was relieved to see her. I hated to ruin his homecoming with all of these questions, but I just couldn't let go of the fact that my boyfriend's face was dented-in when he got home.

"Was it maybe an Army thing?" I offered. "Like an initiation into their group or something?"

"No," Daniel said.

"Why don't you call James and ask him what happened?" Abby asked Daniel.

"Why don't you just ask Michael?" Daniel said, skipping over her question and looking at me.

"She said she did," Abby said.

She was trying to convince Daniel to call James, and for that I was thankful.

"Yeah, can we call your friend and just see what he says?" I asked. My expression shifted to one of confusion and disbelief. "I remember James from the fights in Atlanta. I thought he was cool back then."

"He is cool," Daniel said.

"Then can you please call him and ask him what happened real quick? Or can I?"

Daniel gave me a sideways look as he reached out for a pen and a pad of paper that happened to be sitting on the counter near the telephone.

"I'll write down his number and you can call and ask him, but I..." Daniel paused in mid-sentence as he wrote James's phone number on the piece of paper.

"But you what?" I asked as he handed it to me.

"But I don't understand how it's not easier for you to just talk to Michael."

I didn't know what to say to that. I didn't have an explanation. Call it gut instinct, but I had the feeling that James would be more willing to talk about what happened than Michael was.

I took the paper from him. "Do you mind if I use the phone in your office?" I asked, looking at both of them.

"Not at all," Abby said.

"I'll pay you back for the long-distance," I said as I took off in that direction. "Just let me know how much it is when the bill comes."

CHAPTER 3

I sat in the office at my brother's house. I should have been out there with everyone else, but instead, I was in a back office, playing detective.

Things just didn't feel right to me. Maybe everyone else could shrug off the fact that Michael came home beat up, but I couldn't. I had to get to the bottom of it. I dialed the number on the piece of paper, not knowing what I would say when James picked up.

"Hello?" he said.

"Hello, is this James?"

"Yes," he answered.

"James, Daniel King's friend."

"Yes, I'm Daniel King's friend."

"What's your last name?" I asked.

"Graham. Why? Who is this?"

"Oh, yeah, it's, I'm sorry. This is Laney King. I'm Daniel's sister. I remember your last name now. James Graham. I just couldn't think of it."

I was nervous, and I always rambled when I got nervous. I couldn't believe I had placed the call and that he had actually picked up. I continued speaking, though.

"I was wondering... I saw... Daniel, Dad, and Michael got back a little while ago, and I saw where... they'd been on the road all day, so Michael went home right away, but I saw that you two had a misunderstanding. Well, I noticed Michael's face, and then he told me he had a misunderstanding with you. Something about a pool game?"

I started to say that last sentence as a statement but then I raised my voice a little by the end of it to turn it into a question. I clamped my mouth shut, making myself quit talking, hoping that he couldn't hear me from over the phone as I tried to catch my breath.

"We did play some pool," James said. "But the fight had nothing to do with that."

I expected him to say something else—to go on to explain what the fight was about—but he didn't. He was just quiet on the other end as if he was waiting for me to respond. I was still regulating my breathing.

"What did the fight have to do with?" I asked, since that was the obvious question. He was quiet for long enough that I added, "Hello?"

"That's something you'll need to work out with him," James said.

"He said it was over you losing a game of pool," I said, trying to steady my voice. "He said you lost and you hit him."

"W-well, he lied," James said. He was reluctant yet matter-of-fact, and my heart pounded. It had already crossed my mind that Michael wasn't being honest with me. It seemed like there was foul play, and it broke my heart that I assumed Michael was the one who was at fault.

"What happened?" I asked.

"I think you need to work that out with your boyfriend," James said. "I apologize if what I did made you feel bad in any way, but I'm not sorry I did it. He deserved it, and you two have some things to work out."

"Why?" I asked.

"I'll leave it to him to tell you why."

"Could you please just tell me what happened?" I asked, feeling desperate.

I waited for his answer. My heart was pounding so rapidly that I could hear it in my ears.

"I don't know why you go out with that guy," James said. "Is it just because his family owns a restaurant? Because you could think of other stuff to do with your life."

"No. Why? Why would you think that?"

"Because he's not good enough for you," he said. "Not even close."

"What does this have to do with you guys fighting?" I asked.

"It's why we fought," James said.

"Because of what? Because of *me*?" I asked, trying to put the pieces together.

"I, uh, you can obviously do what you want to do, but I, I don't know how you've been with that guy for so long. I've only met you both a couple of times, but I can tell you're not… that you could do much better."

"Did he cheat on me or something?" I asked the question that had been on my mind. I said it like I was lighthearted, but I wasn't.

"I should not be the one having this conversation with you," James said.

"Who better?" I asked, feeling mad. "Apparently, you know something bad enough to make you beat him up."

"I didn't beat him up," James said. "I wanted to, but I didn't."

"His face looked like a punching bag."

"I just hit him once, but he attacked me with an object after that, so I had to do it again. The second one was self-defense."

"Attacked you with an object? What? A pool stick?"

"No. A lamp."

"A lamp? Where?"

"In my living room."

"You were at your house?"

"Yes."

"I thought you were playing pool."

"We were. But I went home, and he stayed out. He had plans to spend the night with me since he didn't want to disturb Daniel and your dad at Daniel's place. He was making noise in my living room, and I went out there to find him in a situation. It was a situation that made me confront him, and that's when we fought. I could have maybe managed to get out of it without hitting him. I could have told him to break it up and leave, but quite frankly, I wanted to punch him in the face. He deserved it."

"Break what up?"

Silence.

"James?"

"Don't make me spell it out for you, Laney. Just know that you need to work some things out with your boyfriend."

Tears filled my eyes and began running down my cheeks. I blinked the instant my eyes started stinging, and hot tears rolled down my cheeks. I knew what had happened. I could tell by the serious tone of regret in James's voice. It hurt so bad that I doubled over, tensing with the effort as I cried and tried to do it silently.

"Hello? Are you there?"

I took a deep breath, trying to prepare myself to answer.

"I'm here," I said, doing my best to sound normal, but failing. My voice squeaked and I whimpered, making it obvious that I was crying.

I was humiliated. I had given so much to Michael. I had dated him for so long that I assumed we would get married and have a family and always be together. I trusted him, and it was utterly humiliating to have him go halfway across the United States to cheat on me with some stranger and get caught.

"Are you okay?" James asked. His deep voice came over the phone, startling me.

"Yes," I said. "No. But yes."

"I'm sorry," he said. "I'm sorry to get involved, and I'm sorry you're hurt. I'm really sorry. But he's a bad boyfriend, Laney. He might not be a bad person technically, but he's bad to you. He's bad for you. You deserve someone who won't… I mean… unless you *want* someone who… "

"I don't want someone who'll cheat on me if that's what you're saying."

I had been crying, but I tried to get myself together.

My thoughts were all over the place.

"And it's my fault," I said, out of nowhere. "Fool me once, shame on you."

"Is this not the first time he's done this?" James asked.

"No. It happened back when we'd only been together a year or so," I said.

"Why are you still with him?"

"Because there's such a thing as forgiveness. And Michael really changed after that. Losing me really got to him. When we first got together, I could feel him looking at other girls, but after all that happened with Bridgette, he changed. He was true to me after that. Romantic, even. Maybe it hadn't been so good recently, but for a while, it was great."

"I'm sorry," James said. "I see where this would come as a shock to you. I hate that. I'd like to say I was out of my head and didn't know what I was doing, but the truth is that I did. I knew you'd see he'd been in a fight. I guess I was trying to give you a message."

"Message received, loud and clear. I can't trust my boyfriend," I said, numbly.

"I'm so sorry," he said. "I'm sure there were better ways for you to find that out."

"It's okay. Better now than later, I guess."

"I'm sorry," he repeated.

"Don't apologize."

"Are you going to stay with him?" James asked.

"No, why?"

"Because you said there was such a thing as forgiveness."

"Hmm," I made an unintelligible sound as thoughts flew through my head. "No," I added after a few seconds.

"No, what?"

"No, I'm not staying with him. The last time this happened, I felt sad and I wanted to try to keep him, but this time…" I trailed off, not saying anything else.

"What's different this time?" James asked.

"Everything," I said. The word came out slowly, and we both paused afterward.

"Are you going to be okay?" he asked.

"I think so. I'm numb right now. But I do know it's different than the last time. I can feel that."

"How?" he asked. He wasn't trying to pry. I could tell he was just curious.

"I can just feel it. It's like my heart is already back in my chest. I'm done."

"That fast?" he asked. "Just like that?"

"Well, I did get a pretty swift kick by Michael," I said, laughing and crying at the same time. I wiped my eyes.

"I'm really sorry," he repeated. He was sincere. I could hear it in his voice.

"I'm sorry, too," I said.

"You don't have anything to be sorry for," he said.

"I am sorry though," I said. "I'm sorry you had to get in on this drama. I wish my brother would have been the one who… no, I… I don't wish it was my brother. But I'm sorry it happened at all."

"I'm sorry it happened, too," James said.

"But really the only person who should be sorry isn't sorry at all," I added sardonically.

"I thought he would tell you what happened," James said.

"No." My mind was racing, and that was the one word that came out of my mouth.

"Are you going to be okay?" he asked.

"Eventually," I said. "I have a lot of terrible things to encounter before I get okay, but yeah, hopefully, eventually, I'll be okay."

"What terrible things?" James asked.

"Breaking up. Breaking up with him, and then, you know, my life just suddenly changing. Everything's got to change. I go to the restaurant and to his house all the time, sooo... " I was speaking numbly, and I hesitated and paused, but then I spoke again before he had the chance to. "But I'll be fine. Eventually."

"Yeah," he said. "You'll be fine. You'll get a... much... better man... than that." His words came out a little choppy, and I couldn't help but smile.

"Oh, you think?" I asked.

"I know," he said. "Anyone would be better than him, but you could get pretty much any guy you want... and one who would treat you a lot better."

"Like you?" I asked, joking.

"Yes," he said, completely serious.

Just then, my brother's office door opened, and Daniel peeked inside. He regarded me with a curious, cautious, big-brotherly expression.

I had been experiencing a wave of unexpected butterflies brought on by James's statement about treating me better. I was hurt and humiliated, and maybe it was the timing, but the caring male attention felt good to me. It felt so good that I panicked and hung up the phone. I didn't say goodbye to James or anything. I just reached out and hung up the phone, staring at my brother, smiling stiffly.

CHAPTER 4

*"W*ho was that?" Daniel asked, staring curiously at me.
"No one."

"No one?" he asked.

My heart pounded. "James. It was James. We were done. I got off. He told me everything I needed to know."

"I can see that," Daniel said.

"How?" I asked.

He gestured to his own face. "You have... makeup going down."

"Oh, yeah. It was... I just got some bad news about Michael." I didn't mean to do it, but I cried from saying his name. I was angry and embarrassed, and my face just crumpled when I said it.

Daniel came around the desk immediately. He took me into his arms. "Gosh, Laney, I was worried it would be something like that."

"Did you know?" I asked.

"No. I would have hit him myself. But when Michael told me it was James who did it, I knew something was going on. I figured it wasn't James's fault."

"I did too, as odd as that sounds. It's pretty bad that we both assumed the worst of Michael."

"I never trusted him after that thing with Bridgette Miller," Daniel said, rubbing my back.

"I did," I said. "But at the same time, this isn't a total shock to me. I don't know how, but I feel like somewhere deep down, I expected this."

"You're not going to stay with him, are you?"

"No."

"Good. I know you don't want to hear this right now, but I'm happy you didn't marry him."

"I do want to hear that, actually," I said. "It's one of the only positive feelings I have right now."

And just then, cutting through the silence, the telephone rang. It was loud, and I wasn't expecting it, and I jumped.

"Oh, whoa, wow," I said.

I instinctually reached out and picked it up before my brother could, even though it was his house. I put the receiver to my ear, staring at my brother like I was sorry for my actions but I just couldn't control myself.

"I think it's for me..." I half-explained in a mumble before I spoke into the phone. "Hello?" I said quietly as I put the receiver to my ear.

"Hey, is this Laney?"

"Yes," I said, not looking at my brother.

"Oh, well, this is James."

I pressed the receiver to my ear, hoping my brother wasn't overhearing.

"I just wanted to make sure you were okay since you hung up. I didn't know if you were at your brother's, but it's the only number I had."

"Yeah, I'm here. Hang on one second, please."

I looked at my brother, putting the receiver in my lap, and muffling it in my shirt so that James couldn't hear me.

"It's your friend," I whispered to Daniel. "James. He's just telling me what happened with Michael. I'm fine, though. I'm going to talk to him for one minute. I'll finish this up and come back in there with y'all in a few minutes."

Daniel took in what I said and nodded a little as I was speaking. "Okay," he said. He moved to leave.

"Hey Daniel," I said stopping him. He glanced at me. "Don't tell Mom about Michael, please. Don't tell her yet. She's going to come rushing back here if you do. Just let me talk to her when I go out there."

"I wasn't going to say anything," Daniel said. He smiled regretfully at me. "I'm sorry about all this, Laney."

"I know. Thank you." I felt like I wanted to cry, but I blinked, holding it in. Daniel walked out and closed the door, and I put the phone to my ear.

"Hello?" I said.

"You hung up, so I just wanted to call and make sure you weren't offended by what I said."

"No, I wasn't. What was it? What'd you say?"

"That I could treat you better. I didn't mean to put you on the spot or anything. I was just saying you deserve more than that."

"Thank you," I said. "I didn't take it the wrong way. I knew you were just being nice."

"Ah, well, I wouldn't say I was... I was being nice, yes."

I smiled at how choppy and disjointed his sentence sounded. "I'm sorry for hanging up," I said. "My brother came in, and I got startled. I was sitting there with makeup running down my face, and he walked in, and all I could think to do was hang up."

"I hate that you're crying," he said. "I feel bad. I feel like it's my fault."

"How could this be your fault?"

"Because, like I said, I probably could have handled it differently."

"It's fine. It's better that I found out now. It would have been terrible to go through no matter when it happened."

"Well, I know it sounds cliché, but I usually try talking to God. You've said it's going to be terrible, and I just wanted to say that's what I do when I feel overwhelmed."

"I haven't done that in a while," I admitted.

"Daniel said you guys were church-every-Sundayers growing up."

"Yeah, but that doesn't mean I talk to God," I said sardonically. "I usually just volunteer in the children's church and sing Bible songs with the babies. I'd feel guilty asking God to help me get through something when it comes up, like I'm only thinking about Him when I'm in a pinch."

"He won't be mad," James said.

I laughed. "How do you know?"

"I just do. He's not... you should never feel like you can't go to God because you haven't been going to Him. That's the opposite of what He wants. He's the same no matter when you go back or what you've done. I just wanted to mention it because you said you feel like you're about to go through something terrible."

I thought about that for a minute. "I didn't know you were such a big Christian," I said. "I didn't take you as that."

"I wouldn't call myself a big Christian, necessarily. I just heard you say it was going to be terrible breaking up, so God was the first thing that came to my mind. And then you said you'd been crying, so it just came out."

"I thought you were a partier," I said.

"Why because of the card tricks?" he asked.

"I don't know, I guess just because everybody's gathered around you all the time."

"They do that because of the card tricks."

"I just didn't expect you to tell me to go pray about it," I said smiling. "I wouldn't peg you as the pray-about-it kind of guy."

"I didn't think of myself as one, either, but I guess I am. I didn't expect you to call me in the first place, so this whole conversation was unexpected."

"I know. I'm sorry. Am I interrupting something?"

"No. Not at all. Don't be sorry. I was working on my car, but it's hot out there. I needed to come inside and get something to drink."

"Are you having car trouble?"

"No. Well, yeah, but no," he laughed as he spoke. "Yes, I am, technically, but it's not my regular truck. I have a truck that runs fine. I bought an old car to work on and fix up. I was out there, working on that."

"What kind of car?"

"A fifty-two Mercury Monterey. It was a piece of junk when I got a hold of it. I'm working on the engine, and I have a few guys on the base helping me with the body and interior. I'm learning a lot. It's become a hobby."

"I don't even think I know what a Monterey looks like."

"It's a pretty sleek-looking little car," he said. "It's not a dream car of mine or anything, but I got it for cheap and thought it'd be a fun project."

"My brother would like doing something like that."

"He did like it. He liked it a lot. He helped me with this one quite a bit. In fact, he's the one who tracked down the missing tail light I put in earlier this week. He drove with me to Macon to pick it up."

"My brother must like you," I said. "He said if something happened between you and Michael it must be Michael's fault."

"He said that?" James asked.

"Pretty much. I'm paraphrasing but that was the idea I got... that he trusted you more than Michael." James didn't say anything right away, and I let out a sigh that was full of dread. "The last thing I want to do is talk to him. He's not going to take it well, so that's not going to be a fun conversation. I'd rather just write a letter and mail it to his house."

"Are you scared of him?" James asked. "He's not going to hurt you or anything, is he? Because I'll drive over there right now if you're scared of him."

"No, no, no," I said with a thankful smile that came across in my voice. "I have a dad and a brother who would not stand for that. I'm just... I don't know. I don't feel like dealing with it, and at the same time, I don't want to wait. I want to just go ahead and get it over with. I wish I could just write him a letter, though."

"So, do that," James said. "Why not?"

"I don't know. I'll think about it." I was quiet for a few seconds, but then I added, "What color are you going to paint it? The Mercury?"

"Red. Dark red. Candy apple."

"Candy apple's not dark. It's bright, isn't it? Like a firetruck."

"No," he said. "I think of it as being darker, like a cherry."

"I think of cherry as bright red, too," I said.

"Maybe those sugary cherries," he said. "I'm talking about the real ones."

"The sugary ones *are* real," I said.

Both of us were smiling. It was wonderful to discuss different shades of red instead of confronting this storm of bad feelings that I had brewing just under the surface.

"But it won't be ready for paint for a while," James said. "There's still filling, sanding, and buffing, and I'm just learning about all that stuff, so it takes a long time for me to get it right."

Out of instinct, I thought of Michael and how he would love to help fix up an old car, but then my stomach turned when I remembered that he was no longer a part of my life. My emotions were so all over the place that I felt seasick.

"I thought about painting it blue or white, but I figured I'd go with the original factory color. But like I said, that's not for a while. I still have days and weeks of work before I get there."

"How do you find time to practice cards with all of the mechanic work? The tricks and everything. You must practice to get that good at it."

James laughed. "I used to. Man, did I ever. I spent thousands of hours practicing. Now I pretty much just pick them up when I'm around new people. I have a deck on my kitchen counter, and I pick it up a few times a week to keep my hands loose, but nothing like I used to. I would handle cards and practice tricks for six to eight hours a day back when we were on the base in Vietnam."

"I remember Daniel saying something about entertaining an opposing commander."

"I didn't know it at the time," James said. "I thought he was just a local."

"Daniel said he let someone live or something," I remembered the story even though I had only heard bits of it as Daniel was talking to our parents.

"He let me live," James said. "I guess there are brief instances of humanity in war. Myself and two other guys were captured and going to be taken as prisoners, but the guy recognized me and let us go. It was crazy being in that circumstance with someone who had been sitting across the table from me. We both looked into each other's eyes, and he let us go."

"War is crazy in the first place," I said. "My brother barely talks about it."

"I barely talk about it either," James said. "There's really no point. I could spend my whole life living in the past if I let myself go down that road."

"That's still a crazy story," I said. "To recognize a guy you're fighting against."

"Not really," he said. "I mean, I know what you're saying, and you're right, but think about Billy. There are plenty of forms of combat where you recognize your opponent."

"Yeah, but maybe not the kind you and that guy were doing."

"Yeah, I guess you're right."

"We don't have to talk about the Army, though," I said. "You might not want to talk about it."

"If I don't want to talk about something, I'll tell you," he said. "I'm nothing if not forthcoming."

"Then how do you think I should do it?" I asked.

"Do what?"

"I know that's a weird question to ask, but how do you think I should break up with Michael? If I write a letter, how will I be sure that he gets it? I'm just scared to… I'm not scared, like afraid for my life or anything… but… I know this isn't your problem. I'm sorry. I'm all over the place. I don't know what to do next."

"Just call him," James said. "Do it right now while you're at your brother's house. Daniel is there, so you'd have someone with you if Michael tried to come over. Do you want me to come over there?"

"No," I said, smiling. It made me happy that he offered. And I could tell he meant it. He would have come if I would have asked him to. "I've got it. I'm gonna do it. I'll call him, and then I'll go out there and say it to my family, matter of fact. I'll tell them that Michael cheated on me and that was why he ended up with a busted face. I'll say we broke up, and they'll understand. My dad and brother will be here if he comes over."

"Yeah," James said. "Just make it no-nonsense. Tell him and your family you can't put up with that. They'll all understand."

"My family will, but Michael may not."

"I'm seriously coming over there to help you if you say things like that."

I let out a little laugh. "No, no, it'll be fine. I'll take care of it. Why would you come over here when none of this is your problem?"

"Because I feel bad. I'm the one who woke the dragon."

"I think Michael was the one who woke a dragon," I said, lightheartedly referring to the outcome of their fight.

"Yes, he did," James agreed.

"Thank you for defending my honor," I said.

"I, I would do it again in a heartbeat."

CHAPTER 5

—⟳—

Five months later

December 21st (Almost Christmas)

I took James's advice and made breaking up with Michael as unemotional as I possibly could. It was still a horrible evening followed by challenging days and weeks.

It started on the first night when I called Michael and broke up with him. He threw a fit of epic proportions. He came over to my brother's house, and my dad and brother had to run him off.

I had called James later that night, just to report back because I thought he might be interested in an update. We talked for two hours that night, and we had talked almost every day since. James became a good friend to me during all of the drama with Michael.

And, boy, was there a lot of drama. His reaction to our breakup lasted for weeks.

It started with starvation. At first, he wouldn't eat or come out of his room. His mother called me every day, begging me to come over.

Then, he started drinking. That was when his mother began tracking me down, crying, begging me to forgive him. She came to see me more than five times. She went to my parents' hardware store twice and then eventually to my apartment. I ended up calling the sheriff who paid her a visit and gave her a warning about bothering me.

It was a surreal experience, calling the police on this woman after we had been on good terms for so long. She just couldn't understand that I wasn't going to take Michael back, and she was hysterical about wanting to get him to go down a different path.

She said he was going to move away to get away from me, and *did I want to have it on my conscience for the rest of my life that I chased their only son away?* I explained to her that her son was the one who had cheated on me, but she kept recommending that I forgive him and take him back since it wasn't that big of a deal for a man to have a moment of indiscretion.

I didn't go for it. I held firm even though it was so much drama that I could have been tempted to take him back just to end it.

James was my rock during the whole thing. We developed a long-distance friendship in those weeks and it was a lifesaver to me. James was positive and encouraging, and he let me vent to him about Michael and his family and all the hard feelings they had toward me.

Eventually, after the sheriff's visit, Mrs. Elliot stopped calling and coming by. After a couple of months, I didn't get updates on Michael or what sorts of decisions he was making. Eventually, I heard that he had moved to Houston. As fall turned to winter, I was able to move on from Michael and heal from the hurt and embarrassment surrounding our breakup.

My conversations with James were more about Michael at the beginning, but eventually, we started talking about other things. We didn't mean to get into the habit of talking every day, it just happened that way. Both of us made it clear to the other one that we wouldn't be mad if it didn't work out for us to talk. There was no pressure or commitment. But it worked out where either I called him or he called me, and it ended up going on like that every day.

We talked a lot, and the timing and function of this long-distance friendship really helped me through what could have been a difficult time in my life.

But, with the way it turned out, it wasn't difficult at all. Michael's reaction was bad, but it was made much easier by my new telephone friend.

It was perfect, really. James wasn't from Galveston, so he didn't know me or Michael or any of our other friends. He was a perfect distraction at a time when I desperately needed it. I was thankful for him. We talked about everything under the sun. I had more meaningful conversations with James in the past five months than I did the entire four years that I was with Michael. They weren't romantic conversations. We had become good friends who discussed art and philosophy and books and nature and God. We challenged each other and checked in on our goals.

Two months into our conversations, James talked me into going back to school. I only had two years left, and I enjoyed being in an academic environment. I told him that even if I didn't end up using my degree like Michael had predicted, I would still enjoy the process of getting it.

"Well, there's your answer," James had said. "You don't have to have a better reason than that to go back."

And that was that. I began the admission process and was on track to start again after the first of the year. I was thinking about school even though it was weeks away. I was excited and thankful and couldn't wait to get going again. I smiled absentmindedly as I walked from Abby's master bathroom to her bedroom to show her the dress that I had just tried on. It was one of hers.

"Oh, that one looks really good on you!" Abby said, from the end of her bed. "Turn around. Oh, yes, that's the one, for sure."

Abby and her mother both liked to sew and she had more dresses than you could shake a stick at. Tomorrow night was the Bank Street Boxing Christmas party, and we were all going. I did a turn in the dress. I didn't wear much red, but this was just the right shade that I felt like it went well with my skin and hair. It was a cotton number with a full skirt.

"I'll wear pantyhose," I said. "And I have a black jacket that would go with it, if it's cold."

"I think it's the one," Abby said.

I gestured to the closet. "There's also the tan one, and the blue skirt and blouse."

She shrugged. "You can try them on if you want, but this one's amazing on you. And it's so Christmasy with the red. I don't know why we didn't try it on first."

I sat on the end of her bed with a sigh.

"What?" she asked, pulling back to regard me.

"Honestly, I wish James was coming. I was just thinking about going back to school, and it made me think about him. I wish I could see him."

"Ask him. Invite him for Christmas" she urged, focusing on me like I was crazy for not doing it already.

"I would, but he's got a grandpa back home who's not doing too well. He's said stuff about him not being around too much longer, and so I didn't even... I didn't invite him. He knows he's welcome, but I don't think he would come this year with his grandpa getting so old and everything. He's going back home to Florida to spend Christmas with them."

"I remember you saying something about that for Thanksgiving."

"Yeah, he was thinking about coming then, but something happened with that same grandpa. He fell."

"Well, why don't you go there, Laney?" she asked. "I feel like you like James."

"I do like James. So much. He's seriously one of my closest friends. I don't know how I would have gone through all that with the Elliots without him."

"But what?" she asked. "Why can't you go there? You should surprise him. We'd miss you, but goodness, Laney, I can see how much you like him. I don't know why you don't just make the effort to go over there and see him."

"I don't *like him*, like him," I said. "He's my friend."

A few seconds of silence passed as Abby tilted her head at me, staring straight at me.

"What?" I said.

"I can't believe you keep telling yourself that. He's all you've talked about for the last few months."

I sputtered. "Uh, that's not true. I talk about all kinds of stuff."

"Okayyy," Abby said, as if we both knew I was lying.

"James is my friend," I said, staring at her. "I really do think of him as that."

She smiled a little and shook her head. "Then why are you turning all red?"

"When? What? Right now?" I fanned myself, feeling hot. "I'm red because we're talking about all this."

"Exactly," she said. "It's obviously affecting you."

"What? No. Every single person would blush when they get blamed for liking someone. I could blame you for having the hots for someone, and even though you would never do that to my brother, you'd just start blushing just because we're talking about it."

She thought about that for a minute. "Bull," she said.

"No, not bull. He's my friend, and I'm only blushing because it's embarrassing to say otherwise."

"Okay, Laney."

"What?" I asked, because of her tone.

"Just keep telling yourself that."

"I really don't need another boyfriend, and if I did... James... James lives in Georgia. I can't be with someone I can't see."

"Okay," she said, more understanding this time. "I just didn't know his grandpa was that bad. I thought he mentioned to Daniel the other day that he would have come in if you had asked him."

"What? What are you saying? I don't understand."

"Oh my gosh, see? You get so worked up," she said, giggling and leaning back onto her bed.

"What are you saying? Are you lying just to see what I would do? Did he really say he would come here?"

Abby propped onto her elbows laughing and shaking her head at me. "No, I'm not lying. Yes, he really said that. Daniel said something about him coming in for Christmas, and he said he would have if you had mentioned it to him."

I turned, shifting to stare at Abby. "Why wouldn't Daniel tell me that?"

"I don't know. I guess he thought you had it worked out. I mean, I can't say as I blame him. I don't know how to read you with this guy. You get standoffish when we mention him. I can't tell if you even like him as a friend or not."

"Huh? Of course I do. I love him as a friend. He's like my *best friend*."

"Well, I guess you guys have somehow misunderstood each other because he told Daniel he would have come in."

"Why are you just telling me this?" I asked. I instinctually looked at the clock on the table by their bed, as if the time mattered.

"We thought you had it handled," she said. "You're the one who talks to him all the time. I figured if he wasn't coming, it was because you didn't want him to."

"He probably thinks I don't want him to. I just wasn't saying anything because I didn't want him to feel bad for going to spend Christmas with his grandpa."

"If you talk to him, tell him we'd be happy to have him stay here," Abby said. "We have two extra bedrooms upstairs. I have the front one all set up. Me and Daniel will be going to Louisiana on Christmas Eve, but James is always welcome to stay here if he wants to come. I'm sure Daniel told him that."

"I don't know what Daniel told him," I said. "James didn't mention talking to him about it."

"Just call him," Abby said. "If you want him to come, just call him. All he can say is no."

"I hope that's not all he can say," I said, smiling.

"I mean, the *worst* he can say is no."

"Yeah," I agreed. "Do you mind if I call him from here?"

"Not at all. Just use this phone," she said, gesturing to the receiver near the bedside. "You can do it now. I'll leave you alone. I don't see any reason to try on any more dresses. This one looks so good on you."

"Thank you," I said.

But I didn't care about trying on clothes. I didn't care what I wore to the Bank Street party. All I could think about was getting James here for Christmas. I instantly shifted to the other side of the bed where I could reach the telephone, and Abby walked out, smiling at me for being in such a hurry.

I stared down at the red dress as the phone rang.

"Hello?" he said.

My heart leapt. "Hey, you're home," I said.

"Yeah, I got to eat lunch at home today. You okay? You usually don't call till eight o'clock on Tuesdays."

"Is it Tuesday?" I said, smiling and lying back on my brother's bed.

"I hardly remember what day of the week it is. It all blurs together around Christmas. I'm over at Daniel's, trying on Abby's dresses."

"Is that something you girls do?"

I laughed. "No. She's just got a lot of them, so I came to raid her closet for something to wear to that party tomorrow."

"Oh, at the gym?" he asked.

"Yeah. Hey, I know you were heading home in a few days but I didn't know if you… I wanted to make sure you knew you were welcome to… that we wanted you to come here, to come spend Christmas here with me, with us, at my brother's. They have an extra bedroom upstairs, and they won't be here for Christmas, but I, you know. I'll be here. Me and my parents and family and everything. I didn't think you could even consider coming because of your grandpa and everything, but I wanted to make sure you knew you were more than welcome to come here."

I made myself stop rambling and pause long enough to wait for him to say something.

"Sure," he said, after what seemed like a year.

"Sure?" I asked.

"Sure, yes, Laney. I'll come spend Christmas with you if that's what you're asking."

"Yes, it is, I'm asking, yes to that asking."

He laughed at my disjointed sentence. "Well, yes, then, I am. I'm answering yes to that, too."

CHAPTER 6

The following day
December 22nd

I was ever so comfortable in my friendship with James, and yet the thought of seeing him in person brought on all sorts of nervous feelings and self-doubt. I started realizing how much I needed to clean my apartment and how much I hadn't put thought into my wardrobe options for Christmas. I normally just wore jeans and a sweater. It would have been nice to dress up for him, but I wasn't going to wear Abby's dress again. It was too dressy for a laidback family Christmas.

I thought I didn't have feelings for James, but the instant he said he was coming over, I started making plans to get myself and my apartment all fixed up for his arrival. I still had another day to prepare. He would leave tomorrow morning, travel all day, and spend the night with my brother. I probably wouldn't see him until Christmas Eve morning.

I cleaned all afternoon, so I was late getting out the door for the party.

Bank Street was crowded. There were tons of people already at the gym when I arrived. All of the students who went to boxing classes at the gym were invited, along with their families. There were extras, too. Marvin was a famous, well-loved boxer in his day, and Billy was currently on top of his game. The party was packed. It was Wednesday, but it felt like a Saturday. This was the first year this party was happening, and judging by the size of the crowd and their enthusiasm, everyone thought it was the best idea ever.

The place had been transformed. The boxing ring was torn down and there was a dancefloor in its place. There was a speaker system set up along with a DJ booth where Quentin (one of the boxers from the gym) was set up and playing records.

The action was already in full swing when I walked in. The lights were low, and there were people everywhere with music and talking. There were Christmas decorations and lights, and I got caught up looking all around. I recognized just about everyone I saw. My family owned the hardware store across the street, and we were all tied in with this gym and these people.

Billy was a world-class athlete. He was the most popular guy at the party. He and Tess had gotten there an hour before I did. I knew because Abby called me from Marvin's office earlier, telling me who all was there and asking when I would arrive.

I had helped them decorate, and Abby said I should get there as soon as I could to see how good it all came out. Tess was near the door when I came in, and she smiled and rushed up to me when she saw me. She was wearing a red dress. It wasn't cut like mine, but I said, "We're twins," as she reached out for a hug.

"Hey, you look beautiful. But gosh, where have you been? We've been waiting for you for like an hour."

"Marvin said to get here between six and seven."

"It's past seven," she said, wide-eyed and serious.

I smiled. "Barely. Like three minutes."

"Well, your man was here at six, and we waited and waited. Abby was freaking out, looking for you. But then, Marvin said he could go upstairs and use the shower since he had been on the road all day. So I'm not even sure if he's back down here yet or not."

"Who are you talking about?" I asked, even though I knew she was talking about James.

"James," she said, looking at me like I should know better than to be late.

"James isn't coming until tomorrow night," I said.

"Oh my gosh, you didn't know he was…" Tess stopped talking when Abby came up to us. Tess knew she had made a mistake, and she stepped back stiffly with a stunned expression.

"Heyyyy, oh my gosh, Laney," Abby said coming up to me. "What took you so long?"

"I thought it was starting at seven," I said, barely containing my nerves and excitement. "I can't believe so many people are here."

Abby pulled me along, and I followed her. It was dark in this part of the room except for the moving lights. Quentin's cousin owned a party rental place, and he set up some stage lights and a disco ball. I had seen the room earlier, but none of this stuff was on. It looked like a different place now.

I recognized the song that was playing. It was *Merry Christmas Baby* by Otis Redding. I knew this for sure because I loved Christmas music and I loved Otis Redding. It was a song I had heard a hundred times. I sang along with it as we walked through several groups of people. I was absentmindedly singing about *Santa coming down the chimney at half-past three* when I caught sight of him and my heart stopped.

I already knew that James had come in early. Tess had spilled the beans. And yet seeing him there, in the same room as me, came as a shock. I hadn't seen him in almost a year, and in that time, he had physically changed and he had become one of my best friends. It was unbelievable to think that the man standing next to my brother was the same James I had been talking to on the phone.

I definitely had some sort of feelings for him. I felt an instant rush of emotion that made me have to fight back tears. I looked at my brother. I was smiling and trying to act normal as I glanced at him and then back at James again. I had no idea I would react this way when I saw him. My heart raced as I walked that way. I imagined myself running to him and falling into his arms. I saw the whole scene in my mind before reminding myself that I was not going to do that.

James saw me.

He was smiling at me, but I had no idea what he was thinking. He was smiling at me. Oh, gosh, he was smiling at me.

I didn't anticipate feeling all these things. I knew I liked him, but I did not remember how handsome he was—not even close. When I was committed to Michael, I was committed. I could appreciate it when a guy was handsome looking, but I never got butterflies or giddy feelings because of it. Today was different. I saw James's face and form in a different way now that romance was an option. I felt flush, like blood was rushing through my body so fast that I might explode. I smiled and tried to act casual.

"You're early!" I said, yelling out to him as we got closer.

"I left this morning," he said with a little shrug.

His eyes were blue. *Oh, goodness. Had I never looked into them before?* He didn't have a lot of facial hair, but his features were masculine. His jaw was square, and I could hardly look at his face without feeling like I might actually swoon. *Was that even a thing? Did women swoon?* If they did, that was what was happening to me. I felt weak in the knees and distracted, and it was all I could do to keep it together. *Was he the same guy I had been talking to all these months? Did he really have blue*

eyes? How was I supposed to function with him looking like this?
I was shocked by my reaction to him.

"Doesn't she look beautiful?" Abby said, leaning over to speak to James. I couldn't believe she just came out and said that to a guy who was supposed to be my friend.

"She's so very beautiful," James said, staring at me and answering her with no awkwardness at all.

"When did you get here?" I asked since I was too nervous to take the compliment properly.

"About an hour ago," James answered.

Everyone was still standing around, but they kept talking amongst themselves while James and I converged, looking at each other. I was only a couple of feet from him. I scanned his appearance. He was dressed in dark clothes, a button-down shirt, and pants. He looked casual but clean and sharp.

"Hi," I said.

"Hello, Laney King," he reached out for a hug, and I leaned in to hug him. I tried my best not to be awkward even though my body was buzzing with anticipation.

"It's so weird seeing you," I said as we converged in a light, sideways hug. "It's crazy to put a face with the voice after so long."

I was shaken. He smelled nice. He had just showered. Goodness, gracious. He had muscles. My body reacted to touching him, and… "I didn't know your eyes were blue," I said.

"Yes, you did," he said, teasing me. "We've met, remember? And I've said it on the phone."

"When?"

"When I was telling you about my mom and dad both having brown eyes, but mine came out different."

I did remember that. I nodded, staring into the facets of his light eyes. I did know that they were blue, come to think about it. But I didn't know they were this shade. I didn't know they reflected light in a way that was mesmerizing. I could hardly look at him without getting lost in them.

"It's candy apple red," he said.

"What is?" I asked.

"Your dress. It's just like my car."

"Oh, this? I borrowed it."

"I love it," he said. "You're..." he trailed off but then continued, "so beautiful."

I blushed. I could feel blood rush to my cheeks, and fortunately, someone needed to get past me. I stepped back, getting out of the way. As I turned, I saw that it was one of the coaches, a guy named Dizzy. I gave him a little wave and said, "Hey, Merry Christmas."

"Merry Christmas, Miss King," Dizzy said, stopping in his tracks momentarily to speak to us. "I see you've met James," he added, since the two of us were standing so close. Dizzy was talking to me, and I stuttered.

"Oh, y-yes sir we, we... met before."

"Okay, then," he said, nodding. "Well, have either of you seen Billy?"

I started to say I hadn't, but James pointed. "He's right over there," he said

Dizzy turned and peered in that direction before looking at us again. "All right, well you two enjoy yourselves," he said, walking off.

"You too, Dizzy!" I called, like a big nerd.

The Otis song wrapped up, and another song came on. It wasn't a Christmas song. It was Elvis Presley's *I Can't Help Falling in Love*, and the music and lyrics were so perfect with my feelings that it made it impossible to look at James.

"Is this even a Christmas song?" I asked, looking around, and feeling like I needed to fan myself again.

"Quentin is playing non-Christmas music, too," James assured me with a calm smile. "He played *Louie Louie* earlier, and *The Twist*."

"Oh, yeah, okay. I thought they were just doing Christmas music. That's crazy. I can't believe how many people are here."

Dizzy had walked away, and I moved to stand on the other side of James, out of the way of other people walking by. I did all this talking and moving to avoid the Elvis song, but it was hard to ignore the fact that I couldn't help falling in love with someone as that song was playing.

"Are you okay with me coming early?" James asked. "I thought maybe I should ask, but then I wanted to make it a surprise."

"Oh, no, no, yes, I'm so happy you're here," I said. "I wanted you to come early. I would have been here sooner if I had known you were coming."

"I didn't call because I wasn't sure if I'd make it. I thought I might run into traffic in some of the bigger cities on the way."

"Did you?"

"No, it was fine." He smiled and made a shrugging motion that was absolutely irresistible. "I made it."

"Have you been here for an hour?" I asked.

"About," he said. "But Mister Jones let me use the shower in his apartment."

"I smelled that," I said. "I mean, you smell clean," I added, trying for a recovery.

"Thanks, you smell clean, too," he said. He grinned at me. He had an easy sort of confidence that made me want to melt. He looked out at the room full of people. "This is not what I expected when you said it was a party at the boxing gym."

"What'd you expect?" I asked.

"Just... I don't know... a lot fewer people. I thought there'd be a bunch of shirtless guys with boxing gloves, just patting each other on the shoulder and wishing each other Merry Christmas."

I laughed. "Really?"

"No," he said, laughing. "I don't know what I thought. Not this. This is way more."

"More Christmasy?"

"Yeah, more everything. More people, more lights, more like a party."

"Yeah, I'm a little surprised, too," I said. The Elvis song wrapped up while we talked, thank goodness, and a slow Christmas song began—the one about roasting chestnuts on an open fire.

People were talking and going about their business, and I stood next to James, feeling like I wanted to step closer to him. *Could I hug him again? Was that a thing people did? A double hug?* I contemplated reaching out for him, but I couldn't bring myself to do it.

CHAPTER 7

—⁓—

I looked out at the boxing gym, which had been transformed.

There were lights and decorations all over the place, but it was especially different in the back where James and I were standing. That was where all the people were packed in. The boxing ring had been taken down, and it looked huge and open, which was a good thing since it was more crowded than I ever expected.

I knew when I came in that there were a lot of people, but I had been so focused on finding James that I hadn't fully appreciated the festive feeling of the party. Everyone was dressed for the occasion. Most were wearing something red or green or even sparkly.

"We could dance sometime if you want," James said.

"Sure, definitely," I answered before he barely had time to get the offer out.

"Really? Now?" he asked, looking at me.

"Yeah. I mean, if you want."

"I do," he said nodding.

We took a few steps away from the spot where we were standing, and got to the edge of the area where people were dancing. James took a hold of me confidently, placing one hand in mine and the other on the back of my waist.

And there it was—happening again.

I honestly never knew what the word swoon meant. I had read romance novels, but I had never experienced swooning, myself. I could imagine it was a certain, specific feeling that came over a person, but now I knew what that feeling was. I was light-headed and love-struck as James took me into his arms. We were only touching lightly, but even still, there were currents of electricity flowing through me at the places where we made contact.

The Christmas Song was basically over, and I prayed with all my might that there would be another ballad. I got my wish. Quentin went right into another song. It was *My Girl*, and it wasn't as slow as the one before it, but there was no need for James and me to separate. We just kept touching and swaying.

James led me, and I was thankful for that.

The extent of my physical attraction to him was honestly a surprise. I could hardly look at him. He was movie-star handsome, and I didn't even know it. I must have been extremely loyal to Michael to not have noticed the extent of this handsomeness when I met him the first time.

"See, I told you they weren't playing all Christmas music," he said as we swayed.

"Yeah, he's switching off, isn't he? I'm glad. It might be weird dancing to Christmas music."

"We were just doing it," he said. "Was that weird for you?"

"No, it was definitely not weird. I meant, you know, that one was generic. But how about Silent Night… is it weird to slow dance to that?" It was an honest question, I looked around at the other couples dancing and wondered.

"He played Silent Night earlier before you got here, and there were people dancing."

"Were you dancing?" I asked.

"No," he said with a smile.

"Were you dancing to other songs?"

I pulled back to look at him and I experienced a wave of excitement and desire. He was big and masculine, and I felt protected in his arms. I had to fight the urge to stretch up and kiss him right then.

"Did I dance with anyone before you got here?" he asked. "Is that what you were asking?"

"Yes."

"Yes, I did," he said. "A couple of nice young ladies asked me to dance before I decided to go take a shower. I was just coming back down here when you came in."

All those butterflies turned into jealousy. "Who did you dance with before? Young ladies? Who? Were you, like, fast dancing or slow dancing?"

"Fast dancing? No. I'm not big on fast dancing."

"W-wuh, you were *slow dancing* with someone?" I must have sounded as stunned as I felt because James pulled back to focus on me. "I mean, who was it? Were you really?"

"I guess you call it slow dancing," James said, innocently. "We were just doing this like what I'm doing with you now."

"You were dancing with someone like this? Who? Who was it?"

"I danced once with Dizzy's daughter, and once or twice with Quentin's sister. She asked me. They asked me. I wasn't even thinking about dancing, but I felt bad saying no."

Both of the girls he mentioned were attractive, and it was with great difficulty that I kept a neutral face and didn't allow my extreme jealousy to show.

"Are you jealous?" he asked.

"What? Me? No. Yes. I am. I think I am."

My eyes met his.

"I didn't think I would be jealous, but thinking about Amanda or Jesse dancing with… twice?" I said. "Jesse asked you twice? Or was it Amanda that asked you twice?"

James smiled at my apparent frustration. "I don't even know their names. Jesse was the one who mentioned a second dance, I think. We were already out here dancing, and she just asked if I wanted to go again."

I made a groaning sound like I was mad, but then I smiled at him, using the moment as an excuse to squeeze him and hold him a little tighter.

"I'm just kidding. It's my fault for being late. But I am a little jealous. I would have been here earlier if I would have known other women were dancing with... you."

When I started the sentence, I was going to be playful and say something like 'other women were dancing with *my man*', but I couldn't bring myself to call him that as a joke when I really meant it.

I couldn't expect him to turn down those girls when they had asked him to dance, though. He was a nice guy, and he wasn't going to refuse them. And more than that, he and I were just friends. We had never, ever talked about being more than friends. *Oh, goodness, why hadn't we talked about that?*

James leaned down, holding me close and putting his mouth near my ear.

"I happen to be really happy that you're jealous," he said.

Goodness.

I was trying to pick the best thing to say in response to that when I felt a hand on my shoulder.

"Can we steal James to come show our dad that card trick when y'all are done?"

I glanced back to find Debbie and Dawn Carson. They were sisters in their thirties, and they were also the daughters of the people who owned the diner on the corner.

"Dad's only staying for a few more minutes," they said to James. "And we wanted you to show him that card trick you showed us earlier. That one where our card was on top, remember?"

"Sure," James said. "I'll be right over."

They thanked him, and he looked at me again as they walked away. The song was ending, anyway, so our swaying had come to a stop. A faster song started, and I pulled away from James, smiling and giving his arm a squeeze as I took a step back.

"You better go catch Mister Carson," I said. "We can dance again later." I was trying to be casual and easygoing. His popularity wasn't a surprise to me. I had seen him making friends at Teddy's party that time. I knew he had a way of being the center of everyone's attention. It's just that I never knew that I would want to be the center of his.

"How about you come with me, and then we can dance again when I'm done," he said.

I bit the inside of my lip and nodded, blinking up at him. James bent down and kissed my cheek, squeezing my upper arms to hold me in place for a second while he did it. He let me go, and I smiled at him.

"Stay with me," he said. "Come with me over there and don't leave my side."

"Okay," I said, agreeing easily.

James pulled me along, following Debbie and Dawn, and for the next half-hour, I watched him entertain the eight or ten people who were in Mister Carson's group. He showed them four card tricks and a magic trick with a coin. It was a special coin that Mrs. Carson had in her purse, and he made it appear in Dawn Carson's pocket. Even I didn't know how he did it. It was fun, and I loved that he knew how to make people smile.

I had grown up on this block, and I knew some of the employees over at Carson's Diner, but I rarely talked to Mister Carson himself or to his immediate family, so it was nice to spend a few minutes with them.

James and I excused ourselves when we saw my brother motioning for us to go to him. The Carsons had been meaning to slip out, anyway, so they took off.

Marvin and Dizzy said a few words over the mic before Billy and Daniel did the same. Each man only spoke for a minute or two before handing the mic to the next person. Daniel was the last person to speak, and he introduced James as his guest and told us all to make him feel welcome.

James waved when Daniel introduced him, and everyone clapped. As he was taking his hand out of the air, it came down on me. He rested it on my back in a possessive gesture, giving me a little tug toward him. I smiled at him as the applause died down.

Daniel continued speaking, but I could feel that eyes were still on us. James hadn't touched me at all since we were dancing earlier, and I wasn't expecting the public contact, but I went with it, smiling and leaning a little closer to him.

I could smell him and feel him, and this closeness was amazing. I reckoned it was just Marvin's soap I was smelling, but it was James who was wearing it, and it was mixed with the natural smell of him. I had to resist the urge to lean into him even more. The crowd laughed at something else Daniel said, and I smiled just to seem like I had heard, but I hadn't. He could have been talking about me for all I knew. James's hand was on my back, and that was all I could think about at the moment.

***

It was an hour later when Tess came up behind me as I washed my face in the women's restroom. "Are you okay?" she asked.

I had on some makeup, so I was trying to strategically splash cold water on my face without causing black mascara to run down my cheeks. "Yes," I said. "I'm fine. I'm good."

"What happened?" she asked, since it wasn't normal to find me doing this in the ladies' room.

"It's just James," I said. "We've been in there dancing, and he's... I'm... I can't help but get a little... I wasn't expecting

James to be here tonight, and I wasn't expecting to react to him like this. I can't think straight."

I dried off with a paper towel that I took from a nearby dispenser. I stared into the mirror, wiping my face strategically so I wouldn't smear anything.

"It's nothing bad," I added, seeing her come up beside me looking concerned. "It's just crazy seeing him here. I had been talking to him so much on the phone, that I had sort of formed a different image to go with the personality, and now that we're here, and we're talking and dancing and everything. I'm just overwhelmed by it all."

"Do you like him?" she asked as if she couldn't tell.

"Yes, I like him," I said. "I'm scared of how much I like him. That's why I'm affected like this. I'm terrified that I'll do something to mess this up. I don't even know why he's still here, trying to see me after I spent all that time complaining about Michael and not even acknowledging that he was right there..." I trailed off when I realized that there was no use finishing that sentence. "I guess I'm just realizing how much I like him, that's all."

"Like my sister with your brother?" Tess said.

"I guess so," I said, nodding thoughtfully.

I had been mad at Abby when she first came around to liking my brother. I didn't understand how someone could just flip a switch after being aloof. But now I did understand that. It had happened to me, and it was completely out of my control.

My switch had been flipped. I imagined I'd need to apologize to Abby for giving her a hard time about it. I didn't say as much to Tess, though. I just agreed when she said that.

"Yeah," I said. "I get it. I just keep thinking back to the things James told me when I couldn't see him."

"Good things?"

"Yes. All good. I just had myself talked into assuming it could never work between us, and now that he's here, and we're having fun and looking at each other. Gosh, I don't know, Tess. I like him so much. I'm just in here trying to cool off so I'm not so obvious all the time. Don't tell him I said that. Don't tell him I said any of this."

Tess laughed. "I don't need to," she said. "I saw him right outside of here, and he's acting as torn up as you are."

"What do you mean?"

"He said he was in love. He asked me why I gave you that dress to wear, and I told him it was my sister's dress and not mine."

"Wait, wait, wait, back up. What'd you say before that?"

"I don't know, what'd I say?" she asked.

Several women came into the bathroom together, but we just kept talking.

"You said he said he was in love."

"He did say he's in love," Tess said.

"No, he didn't. What'd he say?"

I was so excited and tense that Tess laughed. "Go ask him yourself," she said. "I just asked him if he was having fun and he said 'yes' and then I asked him if he liked you, and he said, 'I think I'm in love.'"

"He said that? Was he being serious?"

She looked into my eyes. "Do you really not know? Billy told me Daniel said he's got it really bad for you. How are you still nervous about it? The two of you have been inseparable all night."

I shook my head absentmindedly. "I guess I just had myself talked into thinking I couldn't be with him like that. You know, with him living in Georgia and everything. My feelings are just all over the map since he got here. I'm so surprised at how I reacted to seeing him."

"Is he staying through Christmas?" she asked.

"Yes." I nodded, rinsing my fingertips one last time and drying them off before heading back to the party.

CHAPTER 8

—⁓—

Two days later
Christmas Eve

*M*y brother went to Louisiana this morning with Abby and her family like they always do on Christmas Eve. James was staying at their house, so they invited him to go with them, but he stayed back with me in Galveston since that was my normal routine.

Daniel and Abby were always gone, but I stayed home with my parents and grandparents and some of our extended family and close friends from the hardware store.

During his trip, James had been sleeping at my brother's house every night, but otherwise, we were together. It was currently 8pm on Christmas Eve, and we had just left my friend Jessica's house where we had eaten dinner and played a game with her family.

They always played a game where they traded white elephant gifts. I had come away with an ashtray and an old, leather-bound Bible, KJV. It was an odd combo, but there was no accounting for Jessica's Aunt Paulene, and hers was the gift I happened to pick.

James chose a goldfish in a fishbowl, which was equally as weird as my combination of gifts. His was an actual living goldfish with rocks in the bottom of a round glass fishbowl. Jessica's cousin, Mark, had brought that one. He kept saying, "Careful, careful, careful," as James was opening it.

"I like my Bible," I said to James as we were walking out of the party.

"I hope you like little Jimmy, too, because, I don't think he's making the trip to Georgia," James said.

"Oh, do you mean I get to keep the goldfish? Is that his name? Jimmy? It would have helped if they would have included some food," I said, peering into the fishbowl as we walked.

James would have been holding my hand if our hands weren't full. Hand holding was something that happened between us quite a bit in the past couple of days. He had only kissed me twice, and both of them were light and fleeting, but he held my hand quite a bit. He had been holding it just now while we were in Jessica's house. My hand still felt empty from when he let it go.

I was officially in love. There was just no other way to say it. I fell in love with him over the phone, and every single moment I spent with him did nothing but make me more certain that it was love, love, l-o-v-e, love.

I felt compelled to be with him. I had to live my life with James Graham. There was just no other option. Nothing else was acceptable. I wished I could turn into a deck of cards so I could live in his pocket.

"If you ever move to Texas, we could share him," I said, joking but not joking.

"Sharing a goldfish sounds tricky," he said.

"No, he'd just stay one week at my house and then the next at yours."

"If I lived in Texas, huh?"

"Yeah. You know, if you ever moved here or whatever."

James smiled but we were approaching his truck so he didn't say any more about it. He had picked me up for the party at Jessica's, so we were riding together. We went straight to his truck after we left her house. I would obviously be in charge of looking after the goldfish while he drove. James waited for me to get settled in my seat before handing me the bowl.

"I'll have to get you some food for him," James said. "I don't know where to do that on Christmas. I guess if worse comes to worst, you could just flush him."

I gasped, and held the bowl closely, protectively, but I was just kidding, and he knew it. I had flushed a few failed pet goldfish in my day, and I knew it wouldn't be the end of the world if I couldn't keep him alive, but I still hoped I could.

"I wonder if I could feed him lettuce. Lettuce seems like a thing fish could eat. I think I have some in my fridge."

"I have no idea," James said. "I thought of a cracker or something, but lettuce might be better. Are you a lettuce man, Jimmy?" James peered into the bowl like he was talking to the fish.

"He said he is," I said, answering for Jimmy. "But you know what? I forgot about Evelyn. Abby's friend. She's got fish. She's got two different tanks in her living room. I could just ask her for some food till I'm able to go to the store and get some myself. You wanna go by there?"

"By Evelyn's?" he asked.

I nodded.

"Now?"

"Unless you don't want to," I said.

"No, yeah, sure. Just tell me how to get there."

James and I ended up staying at Evelyn's for longer than expected. She had some family in town visiting, and her uncle got to talking to James about cars while I was in Evelyn's room, learning about fish. She had some other goldfish in one of her tanks, and I almost left Jimmy there so he could make some friends, but I couldn't do it. I thought of him as being James's, therefore I loved him.

Evelyn gave me tips about keeping him alive, including getting a bigger bowl, which I knew I could order from my dad's wholesale catalog. She sent me on my way with enough food to get me through a week or two.

We found ourselves on the way back to my apartment. It was a place I was renting from a man my dad knew. I figured I might end up moving back in with my parents now that I was going back to school, but my lease wasn't up until March, so for now, I had my own apartment.

I wasn't sleeping there tonight, though, since it was Christmas Eve. I would stay with my parents. But James and I had plans to stop by my apartment first so that I could finally get the goldfish on solid ground.

James knew where my place was and he left Evelyn's heading there. I lived in a large house that had been split into multiple apartments. It was in a nice neighborhood, and many of the houses on our block were decorated with lights and Christmas decorations. I always loved seeing holiday decorations in Galveston. Wintertime stuff next to palm trees was a cool-looking contrast.

I stared out of the truck window as we went down my street, holding Jimmy carefully and feeling content and happy.

"I love my gifts tonight," I said. "I know it was supposed to be a white elephant exchange or whatever, but I scored. A Bible and a pet fish, I feel like it's the best Christmas ever."

"It is the best Christmas ever," he said.

"Oh, noooo," I let the phrase come out of my mouth in a deflated moan as I stared out of the window.

"What?"

"My house," I said.

"What about it?" James asked, looking around with a concerned expression.

"It's Michael. His truck. I see it."

"How do you know."

"I just know."

"You think he's at your house?"

"He's got to be." I got to the edge of the seat as James drove slowly by Michael's truck, which was parked on the street in front of my house. He drove carefully, both of us looking all around. "I didn't see him in the truck," I said as he pulled into my driveway.

James parked strategically so my housemates could get out.

"Are you sure it was his truck?" James asked.

"Yes. But I didn't see him in it. I don't know what's going on."

"Have you talked to him recently?"

"No. Not in months. Last I heard, he moved to Houston and was getting into all sorts of trouble."

James had a pistol under the driver's seat of his truck, and he tucked it somewhere behind his coat. He didn't mean for me to see him do it, but I caught sight of him tucking it in there as I closed the door and walked around the front of the truck to meet him.

We were walking to my house when my car door opened. My car was parked close enough that we heard and saw the movement as Michael got out of my driver's seat, surprising both of us. James put his hand out to shield me when he realized what was happening.

"What are you doing in my car?" I asked.

"It was unlocked," Michael said, staring straight at me. "And it smelled like you, baby."

I felt James tense and heard him take a deep calming breath in and out as we regarded Michael.

"You're not supposed to be here," I said.

"He's not supposed to be here," Michael said, pointing at James.

"Yes, he is," I said, moving to stand a little closer to James, behind him, letting him shield me.

"I heard this guy was at Marvin's party, and I just had to come see for myself."

Michael couldn't even look at James. He was staring at me. He was serious, mean-looking, staring intently. He cussed, interjecting an expletive in just about every sentence.

"Don't you see what's going on here, Laney? Isn't it obvious?"

"Isn't what obvious?"

"He set me up. This guy set me up because he wanted this to happen. Don't you see it? I told you it wasn't my fault. I told you. And you can't even see it now that he's trying to come in here and act like he's some kind of hero. Well, he's not. He knew that woman. He set me up. I can't believe you believe his lies over me."

Michael looked terrible. He was thin and his hair was grown out, and not in a good way. He was scraggly looking, like he'd been drinking or doing drugs. Under different circumstances, I might have believed him. But not now. I knew James's character, and there was just no way Michael was telling the truth.

"Thank you for telling me. I'll take that into consideration," I said, figuring I'd try to take the path of least resistance in an effort to get him to leave.

James hadn't said anything, but I could feel how tense and rigid he was. I balanced the fishbowl in one arm and put my other hand in the crook of his arm to let him know I was undaunted by all of this.

Michael saw me do it, and his face crumpled to one of hopeless begging. He started to walk toward me, looking like he might fall down at my feet. "You heard what she said," James said. "She said she'd take it into consideration."

"It's Christmas," Michael said. "Just let me come in for a minute. I drove from Houston. I thought you'd be at Jessica's tonight, but your car wasn't there, and it wasn't at your mom's…"

"Yeah, that's because I rode with James."

Michael stared pitifully at me. "I've been sitting out here for hours waiting for you to get back."

"Michael, you cannot do this."

"I had to," he said with an intense, pleading expression. "I owed it to you to make sure you knew what a lying snake this guy was."

"All right, I think we're done here," James said.

Michael spit at us. He meant to do it at James, but I was standing behind James, so it seemed like he was doing it at me, too.

"Thanks, Michael, that's really nice of you," I said sarcastically.

He focused on me, and his expression changed. He stared straight at me, pleading, begging, with his eyes. "Please come back to me, Laney," he said.

It had been so long since I had thought about Michael that his intensity seemed completely out-of-nowhere to me.

"No, Michael," I said, stepping even closer to James. "Merry Christmas to you, and I wish you all the best, but you need to go. Tell your family 'hello' for me."

I gave James a tug, letting him know that I was ready to walk inside. Michael saw us start to take off, and he lurched forward in a desperate attempt to grab me. James's hand came out, faster than a bolt of lightning, and he stepped to the side and blocked Michael easily. He held onto Michael's arm with a tight grasp for a second before pushing it roughly away.

"That's the last time she'll ask you," he said to Michael. "You need to go."

James had broken contact with me when he reached out for Michael, so I used the opportunity to start heading toward my house. "Bye, Michael. Merry Christmas. Hey, James, just meet me in the house when you're done, please. I'm going to get the fish situated."

I looked over my shoulder a few times as I was going inside. I could see and hear James talking to Michael, but I didn't try to make out what he was saying. He was confident, bold, and big compared to Michael, and it was clear by their statures that James was the alpha.

I went inside and set the fish and my purse on a side table before heading straight to the window to look out and see what was going on. They only talked for a few more seconds before James gestured to the street, and Michael began to walk off.

Neither of them looked happy, but it was Michael who relented. I watched James as he watched Michael get in his truck and leave. Michael peeled out, causing his tires to make a squealing sound. He lost control and hit a curb. I gasped. His truck shook violently, crossing the curb with two tires before he was able to steady it and get onto the street again.

James stood out there and watched until Michael was completely gone. I saw him heading my way, and I dropped the curtain, quickly moving away from the window. I took Jimmy from the side table near the entryway and carefully but quickly situated him in the kitchen. I jogged over to the living room and bent down to plug in the lights on my Christmas tree.

While I was at it with the last-second preparations, I reached out and pressed the power button on my radio. It was tuned to a local station that was playing a Chuck Berry song.

It was a song I didn't recognize, but I knew it was Chuck Berry by the sound of his voice.

James knocked on the door and I hollered for him to, "Come in!" as I stood up from the radio. He opened the door. His face was cautious at first, but it softened when he saw that I was smiling at him. "Come in," I said over the music.

James came inside.

"I'm so sorry about that," I said as I crossed the room heading his way. He went instantly to the window and peered out of it the same way I had been doing.

"Did you say it was the first time he's bothered you in a while," James asked.

"Yes. I haven't seen him in months."

I moved to stand closer to James in the living room, and he turned and let the curtain fall behind him. He regarded me from five or six feet away.

"I hate you being alone like this," he said. "It's not okay that he was sitting in your car."

"I know that was weird," I said.

"I told him you would press charges if he came around here again."

"Thank you," I said.

"You would, wouldn't you?" he asked.

"Yes. Of course. He won't come again. I haven't seen or heard from him in months. He just came because someone told him we were at the party the other night."

CHAPTER 9

James

"Burn the ships, I say," Laney said, staring up at him and shrugging like that was her best plan.

She was standing in front of James in her living room, smiling and looking like she was in a good mood in spite of her ex's surprise appearance.

James struggled to take it all in. He hadn't expected to find Michael sitting in her car, and he needed a minute to clear his mind and figure out what was going on. He pulled back the curtain and glanced out of the window again, just to make sure he hadn't come back.

"What'd you say?" he asked when he saw that Michael's truck was still nowhere in sight.

"I said burn the ships," she said. "As far as I'm concerned, you can burn the ships."

"What's that mean?" James asked, thinking she meant it had something to do with Michael.

"I was thinking about trapping you here. A man named Hernán Cortés did it. Legend has it that others did it before him, including one at the rock of Gibraltar hundreds of years before Cortés, but he is the one people remember. He and his troops landed in Mexico after an arduous journey across the sea, and rather than let his men have the option to retreat, he ordered that they burned the ships. They had no choice but to conquer the new lands. They had no way back home."

"I've heard of that," James said.

Laney shrugged. "I don't think there's iron-clad evidence that it actually happened. But like I said, now, it's more of an idea, really. The whole concept of taking away your safety net." Laney smiled at him, and gave him a goofy shrug. "And now that I've told the whole story, it seems like it doesn't really apply so much. But I was telling you, James, that you should burn your ship. You know. Burn your car, theoretically, so you can't get home. I know you wouldn't really burn your car, so I was just joking, but—"

Laney stopped talking in mid-sentence because James reached out and took a hold of her. He pulled her into his arms, bringing her next to him in a motion that was so swift she let out a tiny involuntary shriek.

James was ridiculously protective of this woman. He was insanely attracted to her, too. He held her there, staring into her big brown eyes and feeling like he might explode if he didn't kiss her. He had felt her mouth. He had put his lips to it. But

he hadn't kissed her like he wanted to. Not yet. He didn't want
to rush things with Laney, and he had been trying to take his
time, but good grief, she had told him to burn the ships. Wasn't
that permission enough?

He kissed her.

He did it right this time. Her lips were like warm honey,
and he wanted to taste more of it. She stiffened a little when
his mouth first found hers, but soon she relaxed and leaned
into him. James pulled back, smiling at her and licking his lips
before kissing her again. He dipped his tongue into her mouth,
and oh geez, she was wonderful. She stretched up, leaning into
him, opening, clinging to him, giving him permission. For
several slow rhythmic heartbeats, James kissed her properly.
It was an open-mouthed kiss, but it was full of tenderness and
restraint. James nearly shook with the effort of being gentle.
He was in love with Laney King. He was mad that Michael had
been at her house, but even that seemed insignificant now.

It was on to other things. He wanted to claim Laney with
his kiss—he wanted her to know she was his. He kissed her for
a few more seconds of barely restrained passion before he made
himself pull back.

Laney opened her eyes, blinking at him and taking a deep
breath.

"Are you okay?" he said.

She smiled. "Yes," she whispered. Her eyes widened
playfully. "I think so. Am I even alive right now?"

James leaned down and kissed her again, his mouth putting a sticky stamp of a kiss on hers.

It was official—her kiss was necessary to him now. He felt urgent and impatient about it, like he needed to make sure he would always have this connection with her. They were both smiling when he pulled back.

"I can't take it," he said. "I'm going to worry about you. I hate him coming around like this. I have to know you're okay."

"I'm spending the night at Mom's, remember? You could follow me over there, but I'm fine."

"I mean period. Not just tonight. Like tomorrow, and the next night. What if he comes back?"

"Michael's harmless," she said.

"He didn't look harmless."

She gave him a little smile. "You had a gun in your back pocket just in case."

James reached behind him, taking the pistol out and placing it carefully on the counter next to them. He was happy it wasn't more of a confrontation, but the whole thing bugged him. Sitting in someone's car and telling them it smelled like them was just weird. He was annoyed by it, but Laney served as a good distraction. She wrapped her arms around his midsection, holding onto him, burying the side of her face in his chest. In small, soft motions, she rubbed her cheek lovingly against his chest, doting over him with much the same motion as a cat would make. Only it was Laney, and James felt like he wanted to burst from seeing her touch and love on him like that. He wanted her the very first time he saw her, and now here she was wanting him back. She really did want him. She wasn't being halfhearted or reluctant about it. She took pleasure in holding onto him and it made him feel like he could do something absolutely crazy and impossible, like pick her up and spin her on his finger in the same way you would spin a basketball. James wished they were married. He wished they could do the things married couples did.

"Come on, get your clothes, I'll follow you to your mom's," he said at the thought. He stepped back and let her go even though he wanted to do just the opposite.

"I have to feed Jimmy," she said, moving toward the kitchen. "Three flakes, like Evelyn told me."

Laney quickly fed the fish and gathered her things to go to her mom's.

James had planned on telling her goodnight in the driveway, but she invited him inside. Her dad, Nathaniel, was still up, sitting in the living room and watching television when they arrived. He stood up when they came in the door.

"Oh, hey, James."

"Hello, Mister King."

"Merry Christmas," Nathaniel said.

"Merry Christmas to you, too," James replied as they came inside. Laney kicked off her shoes at the door and then crossed the room with her things, stopping to give her dad a sideways hug with her hands full.

"Merry Christmas. You didn't have to wait up."

"Where did you guys go?"

"Jessica's. I won a Bible and James won a goldfish."

"A live goldfish?" Nathaniel looked around as if searching for it.

"We already dropped it off at my house," Laney said.

"Yeah, and Michael Elliott was over there," James said.

Laney glanced at James, smiling that he cared enough to announce it to her dad.

"Where was he?" Nathaniel asked, looking at Laney. "At your house?"

"Yes sir, he said he heard James was in town. He tried to tell me that James—" She cut off, shaking her head like it wasn't even worth repeating. "He tried to say it was James's fault that he cheated. It doesn't even matter. He left. It was no big deal. We just told him to leave."

They talked to Nathaniel for another minute before he excused himself and went into the bedroom. He and Nancy were both still awake, but it became quiet out in the living room. Laney moved around, getting things situated how she wanted them. One of the things she brought from her house was a small wrapped gift, and she went over to the Christmas tree and stashed it underneath.

"That's for you," she said.

She moved quickly, adjusting some pillows before turning on the television again and jogging back to where James was standing.

"You got me something?" James asked.

She nodded. "Yes. You don't get to open it until tomorrow, but it's something you'll like. I'm going to make us some hot chocolate," she added on an unrelated note.

Laney was nervous and happy, and she was bouncing and scampering around like a little fairy. She turned and headed toward the kitchen, leaving James standing there.

"I'm coming with you," he said. He followed her at his own pace and they went into the kitchen.

Laney put water in the kettle and scooped the right amount of cocoa into two mugs. James leaned against the counter, and Laney went to stand beside him, close enough that her arm brushed against his. She was flirting, and it made his chest feel tight. He didn't want to go back to his life without her. He very much wanted to burn the ships.

"You'll love my hot chocolate," she said.

"I thought it was hard to get hot chocolate wrong," he said, teasing her and flirting back.

She shrugged. "Mine's still the best," she said. "It's the right proportions of the ingredients. And the right temperature."

"I'm sure I'll love it," he said.

Laney spent the next few minutes preparing their drinks. James watched her, thinking he wanted her to do this exact thing every year—make him a cup of hot chocolate on Christmas Eve for the rest of eternity. He wanted her to give him history lessons and laugh at his jokes.

Laney sat their mugs on the counter and stood beside him— close enough that she nudged up next to him. She reached out and took a sip of her hot chocolate before setting it back on the counter. She continued moving, turning while tucking herself underneath his left arm. Laney positioned herself gloriously near his chest and came to a stop standing next to him, staring up at him. She gazed at James like she was in love, and he took a deep breath as he stared down at her.

Laney leaned up and put her sweet lips to his. She tasted like hot chocolate. James had just finished chewing a piece of peppermint gum, and the faint taste of those flavors mingling... it was intoxicating. Maybe it wasn't the taste, though. Maybe it was just Laney who was intoxicating.

CHAPTER 10

Laney

The following day
Christmas

*T*wo of my uncles and their families came to Galveston for Christmas this year, so we had a house full of people in spite of my brother and his wife being gone.

Randall and Kenny from the hardware store also came by with their families. We had plans to eat lunch, but everyone got there early so we could visit beforehand. James came at eleven, and most of my family was already there by then. I wished he had been there at sunrise to wake me up. I found myself wanting to spend every waking second with him. I dreaded him leaving.

I had on a green sweater with black pants, and James had on a light blue button-down shirt that brought out the color of his eyes. I couldn't get enough of him. I stared at him any chance I got. I wanted to spend every Christmas with him.

My mom took a lot of pictures, and I made sure James and I were in several of them together. The film would get developed after he was back in Georgia, and I knew I'd be so happy to have them.

Christmas morning and early afternoon were chaotic. Kids were running around, and everyone was in a good mood, so there was lots of laughing and talking and shifting of ideas and topics. My parents' house was a reasonably-sized place, but it seemed small with all the people crammed into it.

We all spread out as the afternoon passed. A couple of Randall's kids had gotten skateboards for Christmas, and my cousin, Thomas, had gotten a pogo stick. We all went outside that afternoon to try them out.

James had been outside with me, playing with the new skateboards, but he came in about an hour before when my dad called him in. I came inside to find them in the dark living room. My baby cousin was taking a nap in the living room, so the blinds had been drawn. There were several people sitting around on couches and in chairs, and they were talking at a mostly normal volume, but it was pretty dark and cave-like in there with the curtain closed over the sliding glass doors.

It was cozy, and I went to the place where James was sitting on the couch. I wanted to plop myself straight onto his lap, but my dad and my uncle were sitting there, so I opted for sitting next to him. They were in between comments in their conversation, and I used the opportunity to cut in and talk to James.

"I got a hundred and fourteen," I said with a winded huff I said as I settled in next to him.

James knew I was referring to my record of bounces on the pogo stick, and he pulled back with a surprised expression that made me smile. "No, you didn't," he said.

"I did," I nodded.

"You were getting like thirty-two when I was out there."

I shrugged my shoulders, being comically overconfident. "I'm a fast learner, what can I say? I wasn't a cheerleader for nothin.'"

James grinned at me. "You'll have to show me your skills," he said.

"I wanted to, but you never came back out."

"I was having him tell Tom one of his stories from the war."

"And he did a card trick for us," Uncle Tom added.

My mom yelled from the kitchen, saying that we should come in there to fix a plate of leftovers for dinner. Everyone got up (everyone except James and me). I shifted to sit closer to him, leaning half onto his lap like I wanted to do when I first went in there.

"Would you like to open your present?" I asked.

James had given me a gift earlier. It was a gold chain with a delicate gold and pearl pendant. I wasn't expecting him to give me jewelry, and it gave me butterflies to wear it in front of my family and have them ask about it. My sweater was dark green and the neckline perfectly framed the small pendant. I had opened the gift before lunch, and I received compliments on it all day—even from people who had no idea it was a gift.

I had told several people that "James got it for me," and each time I said it, I felt all funny inside like wearing his necklace meant we were serious.

I bought him a thoughtful gift, too, but it wasn't as significant as my necklace.

"Do you want to open your present?" I asked.

"No."

"No? Why?"

"Because I want to trade in that present."

I tilted my head at him. "Trade it in? Why?"

"For a different present."

"You don't even know what it is."

"Yeah, but I want something else."

"What?" I asked, staring straight at him.

"What do you think it is that I want?" he said.

"I don't know. That's why I asked you."

"You," he said.

My insides melted, and I leaned into James. "You can have that *and* your other present," I said. My body was alive with nerves and anticipation. I felt close to James, protected by him. I was in heaven curled up next to him.

"I mean it," he said.

"Mean what?"

"That I want you for Christmas."

"I mean it that you can have me for Christmas," I said, smiling. "And the present I got for you."

"What I mean is that I want you all the way," he said. "That you're just all-the-way-mine."

"As in…" I trailed off, staring into his blue eyes.

"Marry me," he said.

I hesitated for a few pounding heartbeats before whispering, "Yes."

"Are you serious?" he asked.

I nodded. "Yes. Are you?"

"Yes." He hesitated, staring at me, looking like he was trying to put his thoughts into words. "Okay, so if it's really happening…. we can tell people now, or we don't have to. Just tell me if you're going to do that because I would want to know if—"

"No," I said. "Let's just keep it to ourselves tonight."

"Yeah," he agreed with a nod.

"But it's happening?" I asked.

"Yes," he said. "Absolutely. Tomorrow, if you want. I'm all in."

I smiled and leaned forward to kiss him on the cheek. I left my lips there longer than I normally would for a cheek kiss, and James put his hand on my thigh.

"I'm nervous," I whispered after I kissed him.

"Why?" he asked, his tone quiet, neutral.

"I don't know. My heart's racing all over the place. I feel like we really meant what we were saying just now."

"We did mean it," he said. He was speaking softly, and his deep voice had a slow, sticky quality to it.

"I love you," I said vulnerably. "Is it okay for me to say that?"

"It's preferable," he said, smiling.

I smiled and glanced down shyly, biting my lip. "Is it preferable that you love me?" I asked.

"I don't know. You tell me. Is it?"

I nodded.

"You want me to love you?" he asked.

I nodded again, unable to look straight at him.

"Well, I do," he said.

"I do too," I agreed. I stared at James with a thoughtful, loving expression. "I love your eyes," I said. "And about a hundred other things about you. I'll have to make you a list."

He smiled and shifted as my Uncle and two cousins came barreling into the room with their plates in hand. They were speaking at full volume and looking like they planned on making themselves at home in the living room.

I moved a little so I wouldn't look so comfortable in James's lap. "That looks good," I said, seeing my uncle's plate as he sat on the adjacent couch. I really didn't care about his food, I was just trying to act normal at a time when I didn't feel normal at all.

"I think all this tastes better as leftovers," Uncle Tom said.

I smiled at him and made a non-committal sound of agreement before turning around to face James. "We're getting married," I said. I whispered it where there was no chance of anyone else hearing, but I just had to double-check. I had to hear him say it again.

James smiled. "Yes, we are," he agreed.

"I was just making sure," I whispered. "Yes sir, I like leftovers, too," I said in a louder tone, turning to speak to my uncle.

I was purposefully carrying on two conversations at once to be silly, and James squeezed my leg where no one could see.

I smiled and turned back to him. "I love you so much. I can't wait to get married. You're my boyfriend." Again, I whispered the words where James was the only one who could see me, and he tried with difficulty to keep a straight face.

I couldn't look at him without smiling, so I turned to my uncle. "We were just about to go in there and make a plate," I said in a louder tone.

James moved his hand, touching me where no one could see, and I squeezed him back.

"Would you like to go make a plate?" I said, turning to ask James but speaking loudly enough for everyone else to hear. "And I love you," I added in a whisper.

"Sure," he said at a reasonable volume. "And I love you, too," he added, in that same exact volume. I turned to see if any of my family had heard, but they were paying attention to their food and not looking at us at all.

"So, I guess that's that," I said to him. "It's decided. Merry Christmas. You get me."

"This is the best Christmas ever," he said.

"I also got you this leather sleeve for your deck of cards. It's really sleek, it's just like a little pouch. I had somebody custom make it, and I told him it had to be thin and light enough to go in your pocket.

"I'm going to use that," he said.

I nodded. "I know. It's cool. You'll like it. My mom's friend, Donnie, made it. He builds furniture, but he does leather stuff on the side. I had him put your initials on it."

"Oh, I'm excited to get that," James said. "When do I get to open it?"

"When I get off your lap and let you stand up," I said, grinning.

"Never, then," James said, completely serious.

I smiled and relaxed, letting my head rest near his shoulder. I gazed at the lights on the tree, feeling the most content and at ease I could imagine feeling. "I'm fine with staying here forever," I said.

I felt him shrug a shoulder. "I'm fine with staying here forever, too," he said.

EPILOGUE

—⚊ֶֶ⚊—

Two years later

Christmas again

*G*ames and I got married right away.

He went back to Georgia after that Christmas trip, but we just couldn't stand staying unmarried. James chose to finish another year with the Army in Georgia, and I enrolled in college in Galveston, but we went ahead and got married even though we couldn't be together full-time.

For a whole year, we had to settle for seeing each other on weekends and breaks and absolutely any other chance we got. It was a twelve-hour drive from Galveston to Fort Benning, and New Orleans was roughly in the middle, so we met there several times.

That's where we were at the moment. James had been in Fort Benning working as a consultant for the last week, and we were meeting him in New Orleans for a short, pre-Christmas holiday. My family had decided to come with us.

I enticed my sister-in-law with stories of how much we loved this hotel. I told her about eating beignets and drinking coffee in the French Quarter, and once she was on board, Daniel was easy to convince. My parents heard about our plans and decided to come, too. We all thought we'd make a mini-vacation out of it. James would meet us in New Orleans, and we would spend tonight and tomorrow night there before heading back to Galveston for Christmas.

We were meeting James at the hotel where he and I always stayed when we came to this city. I hadn't seen James in a week, and I was fidgeting and giddy because of it. We had been married for nearly two years, and I still got butterflies at the thought of seeing him. I rode up the elevator, crammed into it with the rest of my family. It was nearly impossible to contain myself. I was smiling and shifting and chatting about anything that came to mind.

"You guys are going to love these rooms," I said. "We never get one of the big suites, so I don't want you to think it's elaborate or anything, but there's a king-size bed and a small balcony overlooking Royal Street where all the action is."

"Well, that's all we need," Abby said.

"I didn't even know we needed any action," Mom added.

"I had no idea there was a balcony until the lady mentioned it when we checked in," Dad added.

"We got three of the same kind of rooms, all in a row on the same floor," I said. "We'll be able to see each other from our balconies."

"Oh, my gosh, I can't wait," Abby said.

"Me neither. I love this hotel. There's always stuff to watch on the street below without having to get in it. James and I used to sit out there and eat dinner sometimes."

I started bouncing as the elevator stopped.

I couldn't wait. I hopped into the hallway as soon as the elevator door opened. "Bye, see you later," I said, waving to my family.

I thought we would beat James to New Orleans, but the lady at the front desk told me he had already checked in. I left my family and rushed down the hallway, unlocking my room as quickly as I could while carrying bags.

I unlocked the door, closed it behind me, and in one quick motion, I dropped all of my things and shed my coat and shoes. James wasn't in plain sight, and the room and balcony were visible, so that meant he was in the bathroom. I knocked twice before opening the bathroom door.

Steam and light poured out.

James was in a towel. For goodness sake, it was a Christmas miracle. My husband was hard-bodied and shirtless, waiting for me in a steamy bathroom. The whole scene was irresistible. I moved toward him, smiling.

"You made it," he said, grinning back at me as he reached out, pulling me into his arms. He was still a little wet, and I did not care one bit.

"You're as warm as toast," I said.

He pulled back and looked down at me. "You're as beautiful as…" he hesitated, but then said, "butter."

"Butter?" I asked.

"Sorry, I'm too distracted," he said. His blue eyes pierced through me. "I just said butter because you said toast. I can't think of anything as beautiful as you, so I just said the first word that came to my mind."

I leaned up and kissed his perfect lips. I missed him so much it hurt. I was aching for him.

"How's my little boy or girl doing?" James asked.

Gently, he moved, putting his warm hand on my stomach. He picked up my shirt so that he could touch my bare skin, and I smiled up at him.

"It could be both," I said nervously.

"I know it could be either," he said. "Why are you smiling, though? Did you find out what it is when you went to see the doctor? Can they see that?"

"They did a scan with this machine they have. I don't know if it's a boy or a girl, but I found out that it could be both."

"I'm lost," he said, staring at me. "Do you mean it could be *either*? Why are you smiling, Laney? What? What am I missing? Both?" He stared at me, knowing that I was waiting for him to figure something out. "What are you saying? Two? Are there two kids in here?"

My smile broadened.

"Two babies?" James asked, looking serious and intense.

I nodded.

"Are you serious?"

"Very," I said.

His face broke into a grin just before he reached out and pulled me close, pressing me against his warm, damp body. I couldn't help but smile at his excitement.

"Do I have two children in there?" he asked. My ear was to his chest, and his deep voice vibrated and caused me to smile even more.

I nodded. "You do," I said. "I don't know if they're boys or girls, or one of each, but I do know there's two. That was confirmed."

James held me close, being quiet for a few seconds as the news sank in. I knew he would always take care of us, all three of us, and there was no better feeling in the world.

"Well, Merry Christmas to me," he said.

I smiled. "Yep. Merry Christmas to me, too."

The End
(till the next Bank Street Story)

Thank you for reading James and Laney's story!
Merry Christmas to you and yours, and I hope
you are blessed in the coming year!

Thanks to my team ~ Chris, Coda, Glenda, Jan, and Pete

Other titles available from Brooke St. James:

Another Shot:
(A Modern-Day Ruth and Boaz Story)

When Lightning Strikes

Something of a Storm (All in Good Time #1)
Someone Someday (All in Good Time #2)

Finally My Forever (Meant for Me #1)
Finally My Heart's Desire (Meant for Me #2)
Finally My Happy Ending (Meant for Me #3)

Shot by Cupid's Arrow

Dreams of Us

Meet Me in Myrtle Beach (Hunt Family #1)
Kiss Me in Carolina (Hunt Family #2)
California's Calling (Hunt Family #3)
Back to the Beach (Hunt Family #4)
It's About Time (Hunt Family #5)

Loved Bayou (Martin Family #1)
Dear California (Martin Family #2)
My One Regret (Martin Family #3)
Broken and Beautiful (Martin Family #4)
Back to the Bayou (Martin Family #5)

Almost Christmas

JFK to Dublin (Shower & Shelter Artist Collective #1)
Not Your Average Joe (Shower & Shelter Artist Collective #2)
So Much for Boundaries (Shower & Shelter Artist Collective #3)
Suddenly Starstruck (Shower & Shelter Artist Collective #4)
Love Stung (Shower & Shelter Artist Collective #5)
My American Angel (Shower & Shelter Artist Collective #6)

Summer of '65 (Bishop Family #1)
Jesse's Girl (Bishop Family #2)
Maybe Memphis (Bishop Family #3)
So Happy Together (Bishop Family #4)
My Little Gypsy (Bishop Family #5)
Malibu by Moonlight (Bishop Family #6)
The Harder They Fall (Bishop Family #7)
Come Friday (Bishop Family #8)
Something Lovely (Bishop Family #9)

So This is Love (Miami Stories #1)
All In (Miami Stories #2)
Something Precious (Miami Stories #3)

The Suite Life (The Family Stone #1)
Feels Like Forever (The Family Stone #2)
Treat You Better (The Family Stone #3)
The Sweetheart of Summer Street (The Family Stone #4)
Out of Nowhere (The Family Stone #5)

Delicate Balance (Blair Brothers #1)
Cherished (Blair Brothers #2)
The Whole Story (Blair Brothers #3)
Dream Chaser (Blair Brothers #4)

Kiss & Tell (Novella) (Tanner Family #0)
Mischief & Mayhem (Tanner Family #1
Reckless & Wild (Tanner Family #2)
Heart & Soul (Tanner Family #3)
Me & Mister Everything (Tanner Family #4)
Through & Through (Tanner Family #5)
Lost & Found (Tanner Family #6)
Sparks & Embers (Tanner Family #7)
Young & Wild (Tanner Family #8)

Easy Does It (Bank Street Stories #1)
The Trouble with Crushes (Bank Street Stories #2)
A King for Christmas (Novella) (A Bank Street Christmas)
Diamonds Are Forever (Bank Street Stories #3)
Secret Rooms and Stolen Kisses (Bank Street Stories #4)
Feels Like Home (Bank Street Stories #5)
Just Like Romeo and Juliet (Bank Street Stories #6)
See You in Seattle (Bank Street Stories #7)
The Sweetest Thing (Bank Street Stories #8)
Back to Bank Street (Bank Street Stories #9)

Split Decision (How to Tame a Heartbreaker #1)
B-Side (How to Tame a Heartbreaker #2)

Cole for Christmas

Somewhere in Seattle (Alexander Family #1)
Wildest Dream (Alexander Family #2)
About to Fall (Alexander Family #3)